The Big Book of Little

A CLASSIC ILLUSTRATED EDITION

Compiled by Cooper Edens

chronicle books · san francisco

To the little god's magnificent masquerade—as us! — C. E.

Permission for use of the following materials is gratefully acknowledged:

The Little Engine That Could, Watty Piper, 1930. Excerpt of text and illustrations reproduced by permission of Platt &
Munk, Publishers, a division of Grosset & Dunlap, Inc., which is a member of Penguin Putnam Books for Young Readers,
New York.

Little House on the Prairie, Laura Ingalls Wilder, 1935. Excerpt of text reproduced by permission of Harper Collins
Children's Books, New York.

Illustration from *Little House on the Prairie,* Garth Williams, 1935. Reproduced by permission of Harper Collins Children's
Books, New York.

The Little Prince, Antoine De Saint-Exupéry, 1943. Excerpt of text and illustration reproduced by permission of Harcourt
Inc., San Diego, New York, London.

Little Toot, Hardie Gramatsky, 1939. Excerpt of text and illustration reproduced by permission of The Putnam & Grosset
Group, New York.

"With a Little Help from My Friends," John Lennon & Paul McCartney, 1967. Excerpt of text reproduced by permission of
Blackwood Music Inc. under license from ATV Music.

Book design by Donna Linden.
Typeset in Artcraft and Berkeley.
Manufactured in China.

Library of Congress Cataloging-in-Publication Data
The big book of little : a classic illustrated edition / compiled by
Cooper Edens.
        p. cm.
    Summary: Provides a collection of more than fifty poems, nursery rhymes,
stories, and excerpts which feature little things in their pages or their
titles, with illustrations by Arthur Rackham, Walter Crane, and other
turn-of-the century artists.
    ISBN-13: 978-0-8118-5085-8
    ISBN-10: 0-8118-5085-4
    1. Children's stories. 2. Tales. 3. Nursery rhymes. 4. Children's poetry. [1. Short
stories. 2. Folklore. 3. Nursery rhymes. 4. Poetry—Collections.] I. Edens, Cooper.
    PZ5.B4395 2006
    808.8'99282—dc22
    2005028360

Distributed in Canada by Raincoast Books
9050 Shaughnessy Street, Vancouver, British Columbia V6P 6E5

10 9 8 7 6 5 4 3 2 1

Chronicle Books LLC
85 Second Street, San Francisco, California 94105

www.chroniclekids.com

What are little girls made of, made of,
What are little girls made of?
Sugar and spice, and all that's nice;
And that's what little girls are made of, made of.

What are little boys made of, made of,
What are little boys made of?
Snaps and snails, and puppy dog's tails;
And that's what little boys are made of, made of.

—Anonymous

Preface

ONE OF THE GREAT JOYS in entering the kingdom of children's books is that the imagination is singularly free, and, let loose from ordinary restraints, it finds a world of its own; a world with all the weight and importance of something truly one's own; a world of conviction that dares leaps greater than solid reasoning ever does.

There is a quality of mind—receptive, open to wonder—that we call childlike, for it is children who, in their smallness, are most aware of the grandeur all around them. Happy are they, then, who remain small in their own eyes: Like Alice, they will find a wide vista beyond a little door.

—COOPER EDENS

Table of Contents

⚜

Little Jack Horner

BY MOTHER GOOSE

Little Jack Horner
Sat in a corner,
Eating his Christmas pie.
He put in his thumb and pulled out a plum
And said, "What a good boy am I!"

Little Robin Redbreast

ANONYMOUS

Little Robin Redbreast sat upon a tree,
Up went Pussycat, and down went he;
Down came Pussycat, and away Robin ran;
Said Little Robin Redbreast, "Catch me if you can."
Little Robin Redbreast jump'd upon a wall,
Pussycat jump'd after him, and almost got a fall,
Little Robin chirp'd and sang, and what did Pussy say?
Pussycat said "Meow," and Robin jump'd away.

The Little Engine That Could

BY WATTY PIPER

(An excerpt)

THEN THE LITTLE CLOWN called out, "The Passenger Engine is not the only one in the world. Here is another engine coming, a great big strong one. Let us ask him to help us."

The little toy clown waved his flag and the Big Strong Engine came to a stop. "Please, oh, please, Big Strong Engine," cried all the dolls and toys together. "Won't you please pull our train over the mountain? Our engine has broken down, and the good little boys and girls on the other side won't have any toys to play with or good food to eat unless you help us."

But the Big Strong Engine bellowed, "I am a Freight Engine. I have just pulled a big train loaded with big machines over the mountain. These machines print books and newspapers for grown-ups to read. I am a very important engine indeed. I won't pull the likes of you!" And the Freight Engine puffed off indignantly to the roundhouse.

The little train and all the dolls and toys were very sad.

"Cheer up," cried the little toy clown. "The Freight Engine is not the only one in the world. Here comes another. He looks very old and tired, but our train is so little, perhaps he can help us."

So the little toy clown waved his flag and the dingy, rusty old engine stopped.

"Please, kind Engine," cried all the dolls and toys together. "Won't you please pull our train over the mountain? Our engine has broken down, and the boys and girls on the other side won't have any toys to play with or good food to eat unless you help us."

But the Rusty Old Engine sighed, "I am so tired. I must rest my weary wheels. I cannot pull even so little a train as yours over the mountain. I cannot. I cannot. I cannot."

And off he rumbled to the roundhouse chugging, "I cannot. I cannot. I cannot."

Then indeed the little train was very, very sad, and the dolls and toys were ready to cry.

But the little clown called out, "Here is another engine coming, a little blue engine, a very little one, maybe she will help us."

The very little engine came chug-chugging merrily along. When she saw the toy clown's flag, she stopped quickly.

"What is the matter, my friends?" she asked kindly.

"Oh, Little Blue Engine," cried the dolls and toys. "Will you pull us over the mountain? Our engine has broken down, and the good boys and girls on the other side won't have any toys to play with or good food to eat unless you help us. Please, please, help us, Little Blue Engine."

"I'm not very big," said the Little Blue Engine. "They use me only for switching trains in the yard. I have never been over the mountain."

"But we must get over the mountain before the children awake," said all the dolls and toys.

The very little engine looked up and saw the tears in the dolls' eyes. And she thought of the good little boys and girls on the other side of the mountain who would not have any toys or good food unless she helped.

Then she said, "I think I can. I think I can. I think I can," and she hitched herself to the little train.

She tugged and pulled and pulled and tugged and slowly, slowly, slowly they started off.

The toy clown jumped aboard and all the dolls and the toy animals began to smile and cheer.

Puff, puff, chug, chug, went the Little Blue Engine. "I think I can—I think I can—I think I can—I think I can—I think I can—I think I can—I think I can— I think I can—I think I can."

Up, up, up, faster and faster and faster and faster the little engine climbed, until at last they reached the top of the mountain.

Down in the valley lay the city.

"Hurray, hurray," cried the funny little clown and all the dolls and toys. "The good little boys and girls in the city will be happy because you helped us, kind Little Blue Engine."

And the Little Blue Engine smiled and seemed to say as she puffed steadily down the mountain, "I thought I could. I thought I could. I thought I could. I thought I could. I thought I could. I thought I could."

This Little Pig Went to Market

ANONYMOUS

This little pig went to market;
This little pig stayed home;
This little pig had roast beef;
This little pig had none;
This little pig cried "Wee, wee, wee!"
All the way home.

Teenie Weenie Town

BY WILLIAM DONAHEY

(An excerpt)

A NUMBER OF TEENIE WEENIES finally cajole the Policeman into going fishing, and they have a lucky strike. The catch is too large even for all four of them to land. Helpers arrive just in time to see a kingfisher grab the fish and fly off with it, jerking the tenacious Cowboy into the water. Soon the Cowboy hooks a minnow and, with some assistance, lands it successfully.

Summer ends, and so must outdoor swimming. The Cowboy yearns to splash in the sauce dish pool. The Doctor suggests an indoor alternative: a leaky faucet. The General grants permission to go inside and play, as long as nothing is disturbed.

Gulliver's Travels

BY JONATHAN SWIFT

(An excerpt)

I HAD LEARNED IN MY YOUTH to play the piano, and the Giant Lady with whom I was staying had an enormous one in her room, and had lessons on it twice a week. I thought perhaps I could entertain the King and Queen with a tune upon this instrument. But this was extremely difficult: The piano was near sixty feet long, and each key almost a foot wide, so that, with my arms extended, I could not reach more than five keys at a time, and while the Giantess could press the keys easily, I had to hit them quite hard to make a noise. So what I did was this: I made two big mallets, padded on the ends, and stood on the piano bench so that I could reach the keys. Then I ran back and forth on the bench as fast as I could, banging the keys with my two sticks, and in that way managed to play a jig, which pleased the King and Queen very much; but it was the hardest exercise I had ever had.

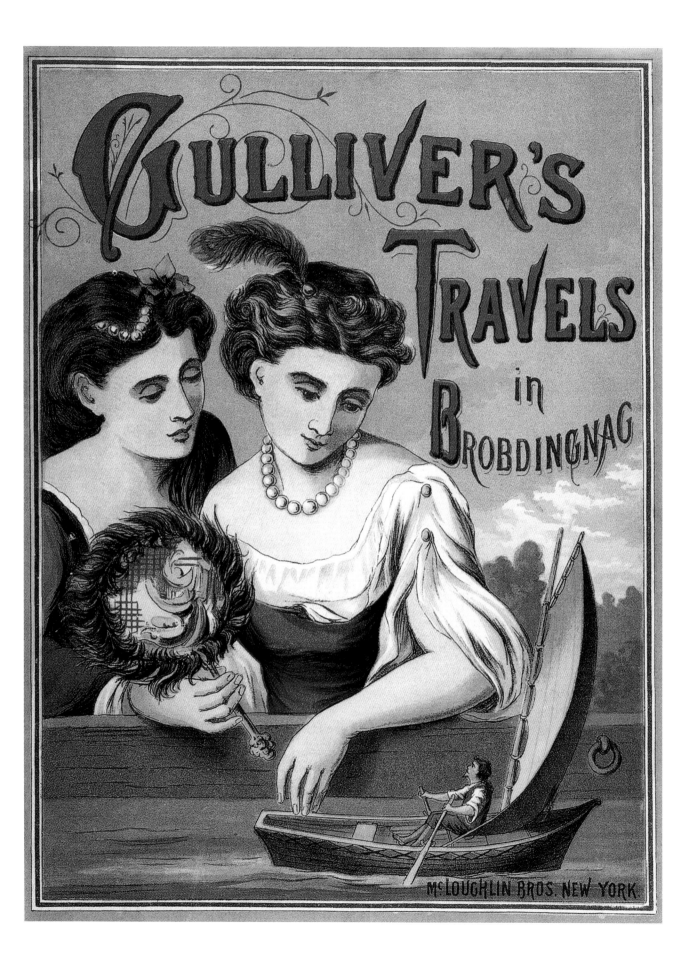

Little Toot

BY HARDIE GRAMATKY

❧

(An excerpt)

THAT WAS TOO MUCH for Little Toot. He wasn't wanted anywhere or by anyone. With his spirits drooping he let the tide carry him where it willed. He was so lonesome. . . .

Floating aimlessly downstream he grew sadder and sadder until he was utterly miserable. He was sunk so deep in his own despair that he didn't even notice that the sky had grown dark and that the wind was whipping up into a real storm.

Suddenly he heard a sound that was like no sound he had ever heard before—it was the ocean. The great ocean that Little Toot had never seen. And the noise came from the waves as they dashed and pounded against the rocks.

But that wasn't all. Against the black sky climbed a brilliant, flaming rocket.

When Little Toot looked hard, he saw jammed between two huge rocks an ocean liner which his father had towed many times up and down the river.

It was truly a terrible thing to see. . . .

Little Toot went wild with excitement! He began puffing those silly balls of smoke out of his smokestack. . . .

And as he did, a wonderful thought struck him. Why, those smoke balls could be seen 'way up the river, where his father and grandfather were. So he puffed a signal, thus. . . .

'Way up the river they saw it. . . .

Of course they had no idea who was making the signals, but they knew it meant "come quickly." So they all dropped what they were doing to race to the rescue.

Out from many wharves steamed a great fleet—big boats, fat ones, and skinny ones . . . with Big Toot himself right in the lead like an admiral at the head of his fleet. . . .

Just in time, too, because Little Toot, still puffing out his S.O.S., was hard put to stay afloat.

Before he could spit the salt water out of his smokestack, still another wave came along and tossed him up again. . . .

It looked as though he'd never get down.

All this was pretty awful for a tugboat that was used to the smooth water of the river. What made it terrifying was the fact that out of the corner of his eye, when he was thus hung on a wave, Little Toot saw that the fleet wasn't able to make headway against such fierce seas.

Even Grandfather Toot was bellowing he had never seen such a storm.

Little Toot was scared green. . . .

Something had to be done. But all that Little Toot had ever learned to do was blow out those silly smoke balls.

Where he was, the channel was like a narrow bottleneck with the whole ocean trying to pour in at once.

That was why the fleet couldn't make any headway. The force of the seas simply swept them back. . . .

Indeed, they were on the verge of giving up entirely when suddenly above the storm they heard a gay, familiar toot. . . .

It was Little Toot. Not wasting his strength butting the waves as they had done. But bouncing from crest to crest, like a rubber ball. The pounding hurt like everything, but Little Toot kept right on going.

And when Big Toot looked out to sea through his binoculars, he saw the crew on the great vessel throw a line to Little Toot.

It was a wonderful thing to see. When the line was made fast, Little Toot waited for a long moment. . . .

And then, when a huge wave swept under the liner, lifting it clear of the rocks, he pulled with all of his might. The liner came free!

The people on board began to cheer. . . .

And the whole tugboat fleet insisted upon Little Toot's escorting the great boat back into the harbor.

Little Toot was a hero! And Grandfather Toot blasted the news all over the river.

Well, after that Little Toot became quite a different fellow. He even changed his tune. . . .

And it is said that he can haul as big a load as his father can . . .

. . . that is, when Big Toot hasn't a very big load to haul.

The Brownies ABC

BY PALMER COX

(An excerpt)

U IS FOR THIS VERY Unclaimed Umbrella which appeared Unexpectedly outside the Brownies' cellar. It showed Up quite Unannounced when the rain and wind chanced to blow. Which was rather Unbelievable for the Brownies, you know.

All the Pretty Little Horses

ANONYMOUS

Hush-a-bye,
Don't you cry,
Go to sleepy, little baby,
When you wake,
You shall have cake,
And all the pretty little horses.

Blacks and bays,
Dapples and grays,
Coach and six little horses.
Hush-a-bye,
Don't you cry,
Go to sleepy, little baby.

The Three Little Kittens

BY MOTHER GOOSE

The three little kittens,
They lost their mittens,
And they began to cry,
Oh, mother dear, we sadly fear
Our mittens we have lost.

What! Lost your mittens,
You naughty kittens!
Then you shall have no pie.
Me-ow, me-ow, me-ow.
No you shall have no pie.

The three little kittens,
They found their mittens,
And they began to cry,
Oh, mother dear, see here, see here,
Our mittens we have found.

Wash up your mittens,
You silly kittens,
And you shall have some pie.
Purr-r, purr-r, purr-r,
Oh, let us have some pie.

My Little Red Rooster

TRADITIONAL AMERICAN FOLK SONG

I love my rooster and my rooster loves me.
I fed my rooster on a green berry tree.
My little red rooster went, "Cock-a-doodle do, dee
Doodle-dee, doodle-dee, doodle-dee doo."

I love my cat and my cat loves me.
I fed my cat on a green berry tree.
My little white cat went, "Meow, meow,"
My little red rooster went, "Cock-a-doodle do, dee
Doodle-dee, doodle-dee, doodle-dee doo."

I love my pig and my pig loves me.
I fed my pig on a green berry tree.
My little pink pig went, "Oink, oink, oink,"
My little white cat went, "Meow, meow,"
My little red rooster went, "Cock-a-doodle do, dee
Doodle-dee, doodle-dee, doodle-dee doo."

The Folk of the Forest

BY KATHERINE DAVIS

The soft stars are shining, the moon is alight;
The folk of the forest are dancing tonight:
O swift and gay is the song that they sing;
They float and sway as they dance in a ring.

Little Red Riding Hood

BY CHARLES PERRAULT

THERE WAS ONCE UPON A TIME a little country girl, born in a village and the prettiest little creature that was ever seen. Her mother was beyond reason excessively fond of her, and her grandmother yet much more. This good woman caused to be made for her a little red riding-hood, which made her look so very pretty that everybody called her Little Red Riding Hood.

One day, her mother, having made some custards, said to her child, "Go and see how your grandmother does, for I hear she has been very ill, and carry her a custard, and this little pot of butter."

Little Red Riding Hood set out immediately to go to her grandmother, who lived in another village. As she was going through the wood, she met with a wolf, who had a good mind to eat her up, but he did not dare, because of some hunters that were in the forest nearby.

He asked of her whither she was going. The poor child, who did not know how dangerous a thing it is to stay and hear a wolf talk, said to him, "I am going

to see my grandmamma, and carry her a custard pie, and a little pot of butter my mamma sends to her."

"Does she live far off?" said the wolf.

"Oh! Ay," said Little Red Riding Hood, "on the other side of the mill below yonder, at the first house in the village."

"Well," said the wolf, "And I'll go and see her too. I'll go this way, and you that, and we shall see who will be there soonest."

The wolf began to run as fast as he was able, the shortest way, and the little girl went the longest way, diverting herself in gathering nuts, running after butterflies, and making bouquets of all the little flowers she found.

The wolf was not long before he came to the grandmother's house; he knocked at the door—toc-toc.

"Who's there?"

"Your granddaughter, Little Red Riding Hood," said the wolf, counterfeiting her voice. "I've brought you custard pie, and a little pot of butter mamma sends you."

The good grandmother, who was in bed because she found herself somewhat ill, cried out, "Pull the bobbin, and the latch will go up." The wolf pulled the bobbin, and the door opened; upon which he fell upon the good woman, and ate her up in the tenth part of a moment, for he had eaten nothing for more than three days before. After that he shut the door, and went into the grandmother's bed, expecting Little Red Riding Hood, who came sometime afterward, and knocked at the door—toc-toc.

"Who's there?"

Little Red Riding Hood, hearing the big voice of the wolf, was at first afraid; but believing her grandmother had got a cold, and was grown hoarse, said, "It is your granddaughter, Little Red Riding Hood, who has brought you a custard pie, and a little pot of butter mamma sends you."

The wolf cried out to her, softening his voice as much as he could, "Pull the bobbin, and the latch will go up." The little girl pulled the bobbin, and the door opened.

The wolf, hiding himself in the grandmother's clothes, said to her, "Put the custard and the little pot of butter upon the stool, and come to the bed."

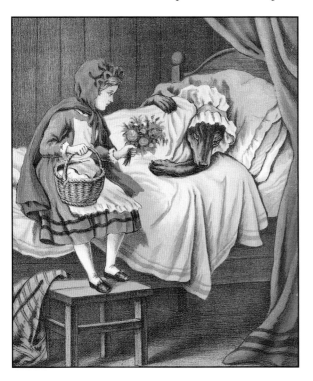

Little Red Riding Hood went to the bed, where she was very much astonished to see how her grandmother looked in her nightclothes. So she said to her, "Grandmamma, what great arms you have got!"

"They are the better to embrace you, my pretty child."

"Grandmamma, what great ears you have got!"

"The better to hear you, my child."

"Grandmamma, what great eyes you have got!"

"The better to see you, my child."

"Grandmamma, what great teeth you have got!

"The better to eat you up with!" And upon saying these words, this wicked wolf fell upon Little Red Riding Hood, and ate her up.

The wolf then fell asleep, but it was not long before Little Red Riding Hood's father came along to see what had become of his little daughter. When he saw the sleeping wolf's bulging stomach, he guessed what had taken place, and with his axe he cut the wolf's stomach open, and out leaped both Little Red Riding Hood and her grandmother.

Moral
If in this world secure you'd be
From danger, strife, and care;
Take heed with whom you keep company,
and how . . . and when . . . and where.

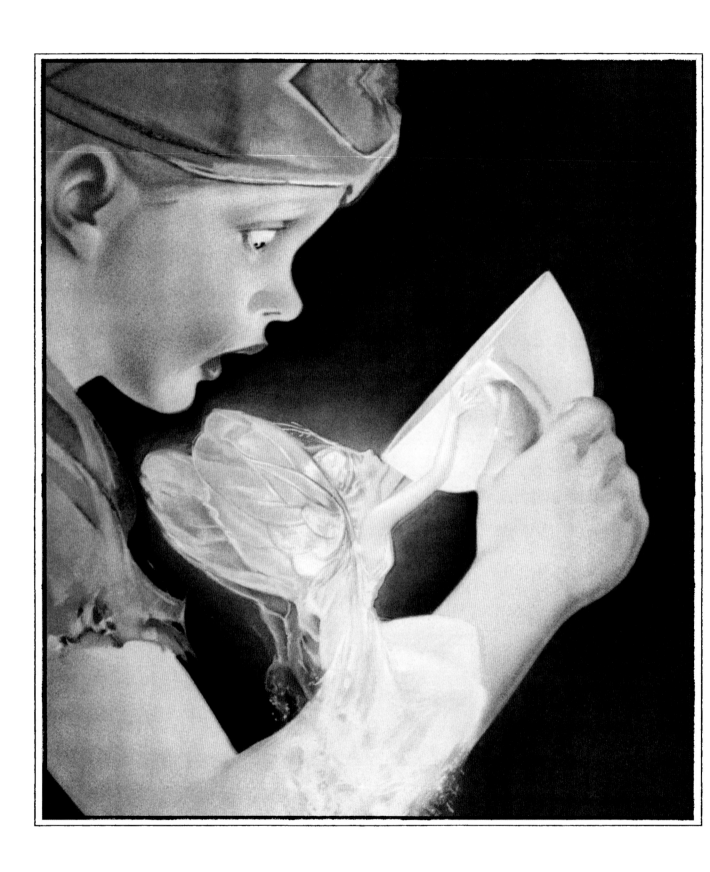

Peter Pan

BY SIR J. M. BARRIE

(Tinkerbell passage)

HIS HAND CLOSED on the fatal draught.

"No!" shrieked Tinkerbell, who had heard Hook mutter about his deed as he sped through the forest.

"Why not?"

"It is poisoned."

"Poisoned? Who could have poisoned it?"

"Hook."

"Don't be silly. How could Hook have gotten down here?"

Alas, Tinkerbell could not explain this, for even she did not know the dark secret of Slightly's tree. Nevertheless, Hook's words had left no room for doubt. The cup was poisoned.

"Besides," said Peter, quite believing himself, "I never fall asleep."

He raised the cup. No time for words now; time for deeds: and with one of her lightning movements Tink got between his lips and the draught, and drained it to the dregs.

"Why, Tink, how dare you drink my medicine?"

But she did not answer. Already she was reeling in the air.

"What is the matter with you?" cried Peter, suddenly afraid.

"It was poisoned, Peter," she told him softly; "and now I am going to be dead."

"O Tink, did you drink it to save me?"

"Yes."

"But why, Tink?"

Her wings would scarcely carry her now, but in reply she alighted on his shoulder and gave his chin a loving bite. She whispered in his ear, "You silly ass"; and then, tottering to her chamber, lay down on the bed.

His head almost filled the fourth wall of her little room as he knelt near her in distress. Every moment her light was growing fainter; and he knew that if it went out she would be no more. She liked his tears so much that she put out her beautiful finger and let them run over it.

Her voice was so low that at first he could not make out what she said. Then he made it out. She was saying that she thought she could get well again if children believed in fairies.

Peter flung out his arms. There were no children there, and it was nighttime; but he addressed all who might be dreaming of the Neverland, and who were therefore nearer to him than you think: boys and girls in their nighties, and naked papooses in their baskets hung from trees.

"Do you believe?" he cried.

Tink sat up in bed almost briskly to listen to her fate.

She fancied she heard answers in the affirmative, and then again she wasn't sure.

"What do you think?" she asked Peter.

"If you believe," he shouted to them, "clap your hands; don't let Tink die."

Many clapped.

Some didn't.

A few little beasts hissed.

The clapping stopped suddenly, as if countless mothers had rushed to their nurseries to see what on earth was happening; but already Tink was saved. First her voice grew strong; then she popped out of bed; then she was flashing through the room more merry and impudent than ever. She never thought of thanking those who believed, but she would have liked to get at the ones who had hissed.

"And now to rescue Wendy."

Little Miss Muffet

by MOTHER GOOSE

Little Miss Muffet sat on a tuffet,
Eating her curds and whey;
When down came a spider
And sat down beside her,
And frightened Miss Muffet away.

I Had a Little Pony

ANONYMOUS

I had a little pony,
His name was Dapple-Gray,
I lent him to a lady,
To ride a mile away.

She whipped him, she lashed him,
She rode him through the mire.
I'll never lend my pony now
For any lady's hire.

The Fairies

BY WILLIAM ALLINGHAM

Up the airy mountain,
Down the rushy glen,
We daren't go a-hunting
For fear of little men;
Wee folk, good folk,
Trooping all together;
Green jacket, red cap,
And white owl's feather!

Down along the rocky shore
Some make their home,
They live on crispy pancakes
Of yellow tide foam;
Some in the reeds
Of the black mountain lake,
With frogs for their watchdogs
All night awake.

High on the hilltop
The old King sits;
He is now so old and gray
He's nigh lost his wits.
With a bridge of white mist
Columbkill he crosses,
On his stately journeys
From Slieveleague to Rosses;
Or going up with music

On cold starry nights,
To sup with the Queen
Of the gay Northern Lights.

They stole little Bridget
For seven years long;
When she came down again
Her friends were all gone.
They took her lightly back,
Between the night and morrow,
They thought that she was fast asleep,
But she was dead with sorrow.
They have kept her ever since
Deep within the lake,
On a bed of flag leaves,
Watching till she wake.

By the craggy hillside,
Through the mosses bare,
They have planted thorn trees
For pleasure here and there.
Is any man so daring
As to dig them up in spite?
He shall find their sharpest thorns
In his bed at night.

Up the airy mountain,
Down the rushy glen,
We daren't go a-hunting
For fear of little men;
Wee folk, good folk,
Trooping all together;
Green jacket, red cap,
And white owl's feather!

Snow White

by The Brothers Grimm

❧

(Seven Dwarves passage)

EVERYTHING IN THE HOUSE was very small, but I cannot tell you how pretty and clean it was. There stood a little table, covered with a white tablecloth, on which were seven little plates (each little plate with its own little spoon), also seven little knives and forks, and seven little cups. Around the walls stood seven little beds close together, with sheets as white as snow. Snow White, being so hungry and thirsty, ate a little of the vegetables and bread on each plate, and drank a drop of wine from every cup, for she did not like to empty one entirely.

Then, being very tired, she laid herself down on one of the beds, but could not make herself comfortable, for one was too long and another too short. The seventh, luckily, was just right; so there she stayed, said her prayers, and fell asleep.

When it had grown quite dark, home came the masters of the house, seven dwarves, who delved and mined for iron in the mountains. They lighted their seven candles, and as soon as there was a light in the kitchen, they saw that someone had been there, for it was not quite so orderly as they had left it.

The first said, "Who has been sitting on my stool?"

The second, "Who has eaten off my plate?"

The third, "Who has taken part of my loaf?"

The fourth, "Who has touched my vegetables?"

The fifth, "Who has used my fork?"

The sixth, "Who has cut with my knife?"

The seventh, "Who has drunk out of my little cup?"

Then the first dwarf looked about and saw that there was a slight hollow in his bed, so he asked, "Who has been lying in my little bed?"

The others came running, and each called out, "Someone has also been lying in my bed!"

But the seventh, when he looked at his bed, saw Snow White there, fast asleep. He called the others, who flocked around with cries of surprise, fetched their candles, and cast the light on Snow White. "Oh, heaven!" they cried. "What a lovely child!"

Wee Willie Winkie

ANONYMOUS

Wee Willie Winkie
Runs through the town,
Upstairs and downstairs
In his nightgown.

Tapping at the window,
Crying through the lock,
"Are the babes in their beds?
For it's now ten o'clock!"

Little Jumping Joan

BY MOTHER GOOSE

Here am I, Little Jumping Joan;
When nobody's with me,
I'm always alone.

Where Go the Boats?

BY ROBERT LOUIS STEVENSON

Great ships a-floating,
Castles of the foam,
Boats of mine a-boating—
Where will all come home?

Away out the ocean,
A hundred miles or more,
Other little children
Shall bring my boats to shore.

Calico Pie

BY EDWARD LEAR

Calico Pie
The little Birds fly
Down to the calico tree;
Their wings were blue,
And they sang "Tilly-loo!"
Till away they flew,

And they never came back to me!
They never came back!
They never came back!
They never came back to me!

Calico Jam,
The little Fish swam
Over the Syllabub Sea;
He took off his hat
To the Sole and the Sprat,
And the Willeby-Wat,

But he never came back to me!
He never came back!
He never came back!
He never came back to me!

Calico Fan,
The little Mice ran
To be ready in time for tea;
Flippity flup,
They drank it all up,
And danced in the cup,

But they never came back to me!
They never came back!
They never came back!
They never came back to me!

Calico Drum,
The Grasshoppers come,
The Butterfly, Beetle, and Bee,
Over the ground,
Around and round,
With a hop and a bound,

But they never came back to me!
They never came back!
They never came back!
They never came back to me!

Mary Had a Little Lamb

BY MOTHER GOOSE

Mary had a little lamb,
Its fleece was white as snow;
And everywhere that Mary went
The lamb was sure to go.

It followed her to school one day,
It was against the rule,
And made the children laugh and play
To see a lamb at school.

Hush-a-Bye Baby

BY MOTHER GOOSE

Hush-a-bye, baby, on the treetop,
When the wind blows the cradle will rock;
When the bough breaks the cradle will fall,
And down will come baby, cradle, and all.

When Music Sounds

BY WALTER DE LA MARE

When music sounds, gone is the earth I know,
And all her lovely things even lovelier grow;
Her flowers in the vision flame, her forest trees
Lift burdened branches, stilled with ecstasies.

When music sounds, out of the water rise
Fairies whose beauty graces my waking eyes,
Rapt in real dreams lights each enchanted face,
With joyous echoing stirs their dwelling place.

Little Boy Blue

BY MOTHER GOOSE

Little Boy Blue, come blow your horn,
The sheep's in the meadow, the cow's in the corn.
Where is the boy who looks after the sheep?
He's under a haystack, fast asleep.
Will you wake him? No, not I,
For if I do, he's sure to cry.

My Shadow

BY ROBERT LOUIS STEVENSON

I have a little shadow that goes in and out with me,
And what can be the use of him is more than I can see.
He is very, very like me from the heels up to the head;
And I see him jump before me, when I jump into my bed.

The funniest thing about him is the way he likes to grow—
Not at all like proper children, which is always very slow;
For he sometimes shoots up taller like an india rubber ball,
And sometimes gets so little that there's none of him at all.

He hasn't got a notion of how children ought to play,
And can only make a fool of me in every sort of way.
He stays so close beside me, he's a coward you can see;
I'd think it a shame to stick to Nursie as that shadow sticks to me!

One morning very early, before the sun was up,
I rose and found the shining dew on every buttercup;
But my lazy little shadow, like an arrant sleepyhead,
Had stayed at home behind me and was fast asleep in bed.

The Little Red Hen

ANONYMOUS

A PIG, A CAT, AND A MOUSE went to live with the Little Red Hen in her neat little white house on a hill. One day the Little Red Hen found a few grains of wheat, and she decided to plant them.

"Who will help me plant this wheat?' she asked her friends, the Pig, the Cat, and the Mouse.

"Not I," said the Pig.

"Not I," said the Cat.

"Not I," said the Mouse.

"Then I'll do it myself," said the Little Red Hen. And she did.

One morning the Little Red Hen saw that the green wheat had sprouted.

"Oh, come and see the green wheat growing!" she called to her chicks.

All summer the wheat grew taller and taller. It turned from green to gold, and at last it was time for the wheat to be harvested.

"Who will harvest this wheat?" she asked her friends, the Pig, the Cat, and the Mouse.

"Not I," said the Pig.

"Not I," said the Cat.

"Not I," said the Mouse.

"Then I'll do it myself," said the Little Red Hen. And she did.

At last the wheat was all cut down and it was time for it to be threshed.

"Who will thresh this wheat?" she asked her friends, the Pig, the Cat, and the Mouse.

"Not I," said the Pig.

"Not I," said the Cat.

"Not I," said the Mouse.

"Then I'll do it myself," said the Little Red Hen. And she did.

At last the wheat was threshed, and the Little Red Hen poured the golden grains into a large sack, ready to take to the mill to be ground into flour.

The next morning the Little Red Hen asked her friends, the Pig, the Cat, and the Mouse: "Who will take this wheat to the mill to be ground into flour?"

"Not I," said the Pig.

"Not I," said the Cat.

"Not I," said the Mouse.

"Then I'll do it myself," said the Little Red Hen. And she did.

The next day the Little Red Hen asked her friends, the Pig, the Cat, and the Mouse: "Who will bake this flour into a lovely loaf of bread?"

"Not I," said the Pig.

"Not I," said the Cat.

"Not I," said the Mouse.

"Then I'll do it myself," said the Little Red Hen. And she did.

While the bread was baking it smelled so good that the Pig, the Cat, and the Mouse came and stood at the kitchen door. They watched hungrily while the Little Red Hen lifted several loaves, each as brown as a nut, from the oven.

"Who will help me eat this lovely bread?"

"I will!" said the Pig.

"I will!" said the Cat.

"I will!" said the Mouse.

"Oh, no you won't!" said the Little Red Hen. "I found the wheat and I planted it. I watched the wheat grow, and when it was time I harvested it and threshed it and took it to the mill to be ground into flour, and at last I've baked these lovely loaves of bread.

"Now," said the Little Red Hen, "I'm going to eat them myself."

And she did!

The Mice in Council

BY AESOP

ONCE UPON A TIME the mice, feeling constantly in danger from a cat, resolved to call a meeting to decide upon the best means of getting rid of this continual annoyance. Many plans were discussed and rejected. At last, a young mouse got up and proposed that a bell should be hung around the cat's neck, so that from then on they would always have advance warning of her coming, and so be able to escape. This proposition was hailed with the greatest applause, and unanimous agreement. Upon which an old mouse, who had sat silent all the while, got up and said that he considered the plan most ingenious, that it would, no doubt, solve their problem. But he had one question to ask: Which of them was going to put the bell around the cat's neck?

Moral
It is one thing to propose, and another to carry it out.

The Little White Duck

BY BERNARD ZARITZKY

There's a Little White Duck sitting in the water;
A Little White Duck doing what he oughter.
He took a bite of a lily pad,
Flapped his wings and he said, "I'm glad
I'm a Little White Duck sitting in the water—
Quack! quack! quack!"

Little Bo-Peep

BY MOTHER GOOSE

Little Bo-Peep has lost her sheep,
And can't tell where to find them;
Leave them alone, and they'll come home,
Wagging their tails behind them.

Little Bo-Peep fell fast asleep,
And dreamt she heard them bleating;
When she awoke, 'twas a joke—
Ah! Cruel vision so fleeting.

Then up she took her little crook,
Determined for to find them;
What was her joy to behold them nigh,
Wagging their tails behind them.

Chicken Little

ANONYMOUS

ONE MORNING, AN ACORN FELL on Chicken Little's head. Plop!

Chicken Little looked up. "The sky is falling," he cheeped. "I must tell the King!"

"Hello," clucked Henny Penny. "Where are you going in such a hurry?"

"The sky is falling," cheeped Chicken Little, "and I must tell the King."

"Then I will trot with you," clucked Henny Penny.

So off they went. And they went along, and they went along.

"Hello," crowed Cocky Locky. "Where are you going in such a hurry?"

"The sky is falling," cheeped Chicken Little, "and I must tell the King."

"Then I will strut with you," crowed Cocky Locky.

So off they went. And they went along, and they went along.

"Hello," quacked Ducky Lucky. "Where are you going in such a hurry?"

"The sky is falling," cheeped Chicken Little, "and I must tell the King."

"Then I will waddle with you," quacked Ducky Lucky.

So off they went. And they went along, and they went along.

"Hello," gaggled Drakey Lakey. "Where are you going in such a hurry?"

"The sky is falling," cheeped Chicken Little, "and I must tell the King."

"Then I will toddle with you," gaggled Drakey Lakey.

So off they went. And they went along, and they went along.

"Hello," honked Goosey Loosey. "Where are you going in such a hurry?"

"The sky is falling," cheeped Chicken Little, "and I must tell the King."

"Then I will jog with you," honked Goosey Loosey.

So off they went. And they went along, and they went along.

"Hello," gobbled Turkey Lurkey. "Where are you going in such a hurry?"

"The sky is falling," cheeped Chicken Little, "and I must tell the King."

"Then I will march with you," gobbled Turkey Lurkey.

So off they went. And they went along, and they went along.

"Hello," growled Foxy Loxy. "Where are you going in such a hurry?"

"The sky is falling," cheeped Chicken Little, "and I must tell the King."

"Come with me," growled Foxy Loxy. "I'll take you to the King."

So Chicken Little, Henny Penny, Cocky Locky, Ducky Lucky, Drakey Lakey, Goosey Loosey, and Turkey Lurkey followed Foxy Loxy straight into his lair—and never came out again.

And Chicken Little never told the King the sky was falling.

The Elfman

BY JOHN KENDRICK BANGS

I met a little Elfman once,
Down where the lilies blow,
I asked him why he was so small,
And why he didn't grow.

He slightly frowned, and with his eye,
He looked me through and through,
"I'm just as big for me," said he,
"As you are big for you!"

Little Lord Fauntleroy

BY FRANCES HODGSON BURNETT

(An excerpt)

"WELL," SAID DICK SOLEMNLY afterward, "she's the daisiest gal I ever saw! She's—
well, she's just daisy, that's what she is, no mistake!"

Everybody looked after Miss Herbert as she passed, and everyone looked
after Little Lord Fauntleroy. And the sun shone and the flags fluttered and the
games were played and dances danced, and as the gaieties went on the joyous
afternoon passed, and his little lordship was simply radiantly happy.

The whole world seemed beautiful to him.

The Little Prince

BY ANTOINE DE SAINT-EXUPÉRY

(An excerpt)

SO I LIVED ALL ALONE, without anyone I could really talk to, until I had made a crash landing in the Sahara Desert six years ago. Something in my plane's engine had broken, and since I had neither a mechanic, nor passengers in the plane with me, I was preparing to undertake the difficult repair job by myself. For me it was a matter of life or death: I had only enough drinking water for eight days.

The first night, then, I went to sleep on the sand a thousand miles from any inhabited country. I was more isolated than a man shipwrecked on a raft in the middle of the ocean. So you can imagine my surprise when I was awakened at daybreak by a funny little voice saying, "Please . . . draw me a sheep. . . ."

"What?"

"Draw me a sheep. . . ."

I leaped up as if I had been struck by lightning. I rubbed my eyes hard. I stared. And I saw an extraordinary little fellow staring back at me very seriously. Here is the best portrait I managed to make of him, later on. But of course my drawing is much less attractive than my model. This is not my fault. My career as a painter was discouraged at the age of six by the grown-ups, and I had never learned to draw anything except boa constrictors outside and inside.

So I stared wide-eyed at this apparition. Don't forget that I was a thousand miles from any inhabited territory. Yet this little fellow seemed to be neither lost nor dying of exhaustion, hunger, or thirst, nor did he seem scared to death. There was nothing in his appearance that suggested a child lost in the middle of the desert a thousand miles from any inhabited territory. When I finally managed to speak, I asked him, "But . . . what are you doing here?"

And then he repeated, very slowly and very seriously, "Please . . . draw me a sheep. . . ."

In the face of an overpowering mystery, you don't dare disobey. Absurd as it seemed, a thousand miles from all inhabited regions and in danger of death, I took a scrap of paper and a pen out of my pocket. But then I remembered that I had mostly studied geography, history, arithmetic, and grammar, and I told the little fellow (rather crossly) that I didn't know how to draw.

He replied, "That doesn't matter. Draw me a sheep."

Since I had never drawn a sheep, I made him one of the only two drawings I knew how to make—the one of the boa constrictor from outside. And I was astounded to hear the little fellow answer:

"No! No! I don't want an elephant inside a boa constrictor. A boa constrictor is very dangerous, and an elephant would get in the way. Where I live, everything is very small. I need a sheep. Draw me a sheep."

So then I made a drawing.

He looked at it carefully, and then said, "No. This one is already quite sick. Make another."

I made another drawing. My friend gave me a kind, indulgent smile.

"You can see for yourself . . . that's not a sheep, it's a ram. It has horns. . . ."

So I made my third drawing, but it was rejected, like the others.

"This one's too old. I want a sheep that will live a long time."

So then, impatiently, since I was in a hurry to start work on my engine, I scribbled this drawing, and added, "This is just the crate. The sheep you want is inside."

But I was amazed to see my young critic's face light up. "That's just the kind I wanted! Do you think this sheep will need a lot of grass?"

"Why?"

"Because where I live everything is very small. . . ."

"There's sure to be enough. I've given you a very small sheep."

He bent over the drawing. "Not so small as all that . . . Look! He's gone to sleep. . . ."

And that's how I made the acquaintance of The Little Prince.

Alice's Adventures in Wonderland

BY LEWIS CARROLL

(An excerpt)

"ARE YOU CONTENT NOW?" said the Caterpillar.

"Well, I should like to be a little larger, sir, if you wouldn't mind," said Alice. "Three inches is such a wretched height to be."

"It is a very good height indeed!" said the Caterpillar angrily, rearing itself upright as it spoke (it was exactly three inches high).

"But I'm not used to it!" pleaded poor Alice in a piteous tone. And she thought to herself, "I wish the creatures wouldn't be so easily offended!"

"You'll get used to it in time," said the Caterpillar, and it put the hookah into its mouth, and began smoking again.

This time Alice waited patiently until it chose to speak again. In a minute or two the Caterpillar took the hookah out of his mouth, and yawned once or twice, and shook itself. Then it got down off the mushroom, and crawled away into the grass, merely remarking, as it went, "One side will make you grow taller, and the other side will make you grow shorter."

"One side of what? The other side of what?" thought Alice to herself.

"Of the mushroom," said the Caterpillar, just as if she had asked it aloud; and in another moment it was out of sight.

Little Tee Wee

BY JOHN HEARD

Little Tee Wee,
He went to sea
In an open boat;
And while afloat
The little boat bended,
And my story's ended.

The Three Little Pigs

ANONYMOUS

ONCE UPON A TIME there was an old pig with three little pigs, and as she had not enough to keep them, she sent them out to seek their fortune. The first that went off met a man with a bundle of straw, and said to him, "Please, man, give me that straw to build me a house," which the man did, and the little pig built a house with it.

The second little pig met a man with a bundle of sticks, and said, "Please, man, give me those sticks to build a house," which the man did, and the pig built his house.

The third little pig met a man with a load of bricks, and said, "Please, man, give me those bricks to build a house with," so the man gave him the bricks, and he built his house with them.

Presently a wolf came to the first little pig's house, and knocked at the door, and said, "Little pig, little pig, let me come in."

To which the pig answered, "No, not by the hair of my chinny chin chin."

The wolf then answered, "Then I'll huff, and I'll puff, and I'll blow your house in!"

So he huffed and he puffed, and he blew his house in, and the little pig only just escaped, and ran quickly to the second pig's house.

Hard on his heels came the wolf, who knocked at the door and said, "Little pig, little pig, let me come in,"

"No, not by the hair of my chinny chin chin!" said the second little pig.

"Then I'll huff, and I'll puff, and I'll blow your house in!"

So he huffed, and he puffed, and he puffed, and he huffed, and at last he blew the house down, and the two little pigs inside only just escaped, and ran quickly to the third little pig's house.

Right behind them came the wolf, and he knocked hard on the door, and said, "Little pig, little pig, let me come in!"

"No, not by the hair of my chinny chin chin!" replied the third little pig.

"Then I'll huff, and I'll puff, and I'll blow your house in!"

Well, he huffed, and he puffed, and he huffed, and he puffed, and he puffed, and he huffed; but he could not, with all his huffing and puffing, blow the house down, so he said, "Oh, little pigs, I know where there is a nice field of turnips."

"Where?" said the first little pig.

"Oh, in Mrs. Smith's field, and if you will be ready tomorrow morning I will call for you, and we will go together and get some dinner."

"Very well," said the first little pig, "I will be ready. What time do you mean to go?"

"Oh, at six o'clock."

Well, the first little pig got up at five, and got the turnips before the wolf came. The wolf arrived at six, and said, "Little pig, are you ready?"

The first little pig replied, "Ready! I have been, and come back again, and got a nice potful for dinner."

The wolf felt very angry at this, but thought that he would get the little pigs somehow or other, so he said, "Little pigs, I know where there is a nice apple tree."

"Where?" said the second little pig.

"Down at Merry Garden," replied the wolf, "and if you will not deceive me I will come for you, at five o'clock tomorrow morning, and we will go together and get some apples."

Well, the second little pig bustled up the next morning at four o'clock, and went off for the apples, hoping to get back before the wolf came; but the little pig had further to go, and had to climb the tree, so that just as he was coming down from it, he saw the wolf coming, and as you may suppose, this frightened him very much.

When the wolf came up he said, "Little pig, what are you doing here before me? Are they nice apples?"

"Yes, very," said the little pig. "I will throw you down one." And he threw it so far that, while the wolf was going to pick it up, the little pig jumped down and ran home.

The next day the wolf came again, and said to the little pigs, "Little pigs, there is a fair at Shanklin this afternoon. Will you go?"

"Oh yes," said the third little pig, "I will go. What time shall you be ready?"

"At three," said the wolf. So the third little pig went off before the time, and got to the fair, and bought a butter churn, which he was going home with, when he saw the wolf coming. Then he could not tell what to do. So he got into the churn to hide, and by so doing tipped it over, and it rolled down the hill with the pig in it, which frightened the wolf so much that he ran home without going to the fair.

He went to the little pigs' house, and told them how frightened he had been by the great round thing which had came down the hill past him. Then the third little pig said, "Ha! I frightened you then. I had been to the fair and bought a butter churn, and when I saw you, I got into it and rolled down the hill!"

Then the wolf was very angry indeed, and declared he would eat up all three of the little pigs, and that he would get down the chimney after them.

When the little pigs saw what he was about, the first little pig hung up a pot full of water, and the second made a blazing fire, and the wolf came down the chimney and fell straight into the pot. The third little pig had the cover on the pot in an instant, and that was the end of the wolf! And the three little pigs lived happily ever after.

Peter, Peter, Pumpkin Eater

BY MOTHER GOOSE

Peter, Peter, pumpkin eater,
Had a wife and couldn't keep her;
He put her in a pumpkin shell,
And there he kept her very well.

Tom Thumb

BY RICHARD JOHNSON

ONCE UPON A TIME a great magician went out for a walk, and becoming very tired, asked leave to rest at a laborer's cottage. The man and his wife brought him food and drink, and he, wishing to reward them, asked them what they would most like to have. "Well, Sir," said the laborer, "we have no children, and if we had a son no bigger than my thumb, we would be very proud and happy."

"You shall have your wish," said the magician, and when he left them, he went to a fairy to ask her aid in keeping his promise. The fairy agreed to assist him.

One day she brought to the wife a tiny baby boy, just the size of her husband's thumb, and told her he was to be called Tom Thumb.

The parents were delighted and soon became very fond of him, but as he never grew any bigger, his father began to fear that Tom would not be able to defend himself from attacks of larger boys. But it was soon plain that what the tiny chap lacked in strength, he made up in cunning. Master Tom used to play cherrystones with the other boys, and when he had lost all he had, he would creep into the bags of the others and steal back all his losings. At last he was caught in the act, and an ugly boy drew the strings of the bag so tightly around Tom's neck that he was nearly strangled. When he released him he was glad "to promise to play fair" the next time.

One day his mother was making a batter pudding, and Tom climbed to the edge of the bowl to look in, but his foot slipped, and into the batter he went head foremost. His mother was looking another way, so did not see Tom and stirred him along with the batter into the pudding bag, and put it into the pot to boil. When the water grew hot, he began to kick and plunge so hard that the lid of the pot flew off. His mother, seeing the pudding behave so strangely, thought it must be bewitched and so threw it out of doors.

A poor tinker, who was passing at the time, picked up the pudding and sat down by the wayside to eat it. At this Tom began to cry, "Let me out! Let me out!" The tinker was so frightened that he flung the pudding over the hedge and

TOM THUMB.

Kringle
ES.

Copyrighted 1897 by
McLoughlin Bros New York

ran away. Tom ran home to his mother, who, with a great deal of trouble, washed off the batter.

Not long after, his mother took him with her to milk the cow, and as it was a windy day, she tied him to a thistle with a bit of thread. The cow bit off the thistle, and all at once Tom found himself in a big red cave, with two rows of white pillars, going *champ! champ!*

Tom roared at the top of his little voice for his mother. "Where are you, my dear son," cried the good woman in great alarm.

"Here, in the red cow's mouth," cried Tom. The mother wept and wrung her hands, for she thought he would be killed, but the cow opened her mouth and dropped him out on the grass without hurting him at all.

His father sometimes took Tom with him when he went to plough, and gave him a barley-straw whip to drive the horses. He felt very grand and would hallo, and crack his whip in fine style. One day, a raven hovering near picked up the barley-straw whip and Tom together; luckily, the raven dropped Tom on the terrace of the giant Grumbo's castle.

Soon old Grumbo came on the terrace for a walk, and seeing Master Tom, picked him up and swallowed him as if he had been a pill. Tom made the

greedy giant so sick that he opened his mouth, and Tom came flying out, over the terrace into the sea, where a big fish swallowed him. It was a fine fish when caught, and was bought for the table of King Arthur. The cook took a knife to open it, and what was her surprise when Tom popped up his head, and politely said, "How d'ye do, ma'am?" It was soon known that a wee knight had come to court, and the King made him his dwarf, and the whole court thought him the funniest and merriest little fellow that had ever been seen there. The King asked Tom about his parents, and Tom told him they were poor people, and that he should like to see them again.

The King gave him leave to visit then and take them as much money as he could carry. The poor little fellow could only carry a silver three-penny piece. His parents were glad to see him, but when he had stayed three days he thought he ought to return. His mother, who was sorry to part with him, made a little parachute of paper and string, and tying Tom to it, tossed him away into the air toward the King's palace. Instead, the wind sent him to the court, and he fell into a bowl of broth that the royal cook was carrying across the courtyard. The bowl was dropped and broken. The cook in a rage picked up Tom, and ran with him to the King, and charged him with jumping into the royal broth, out of mere mischief. The King was angry, but very busy, and ordered Tom to be kept under arrest till he had more leisure. He was shut in a mousetrap for a week; at the end of the week the King's anger was gone, and he ordered Tom a new suit of clothes, and a good-sized mouse to ride on.

One day when Tom was riding past a farmhouse, a large cat, seeing the mouse, rushed out upon it. Tom drew his sword and defended himself bravely, until King Arthur and his followers came up, but he was so seriously wounded that his life was despaired of.

The Queen of the Fairies bore Tom away to fairyland, and kept him several years. When he returned to court, King Arthur was dead, but Tom was cordially welcomed by his successor, King Thunston. Here he spent many happy years and met with many wonderful adventures. But I must tell of poor little Tom's death.

One day he was attacked by an immense spider, and although Tom succeeded in killing him, the spider's poisonous breath was too much for the brave little hero, and he fell into a wasting sickness from which he never recovered.

A neat little slab was raised to his memory, and this was part of the epitaph—

HERE LIES TOM THUMB, KING ARTHUR'S KNIGHT
WHO DIED BY A CRUEL SPIDER'S BITE!

Little House on the Prairie

BY LAURA INGALLS WILDER

(An excerpt)

IN ONE DAY MR. EDWARDS and Pa built those walls as high as Pa wanted them. They joked and sang while they worked, and their axes made the chips fly.

On top of the walls they set up a skeleton roof of slender poles. Then in the south wall they cut a tall hole for a door, and in the west wall and the east wall they cut square holes for windows.

Laura couldn't wait to see the inside of the house. As soon as the tall hole was cut, she ran inside. Everything was striped there. Stripes of sunshine came through the cracks in the west wall, and stripes of shadow came down from the poles overhead. The stripes of shade and sunshine were all across Laura's hands and her arms and her bare feet. And through the cracks between the logs she could see stripes of the prairie mixed with the sweet smell of cut wood.

Then, as Pa cut away the logs to make the window hole in the west wall, chunks of sunshine came in. When he finished, a big block of sunshine lay on the ground inside the house.

Around the door hole and the window holes, Pa and Mr. Edwards nailed thin slabs against the cut ends of the logs. And the house was finished, all but the roof. The walls were solid and the house was large, much larger than the tent. It was a nice house.

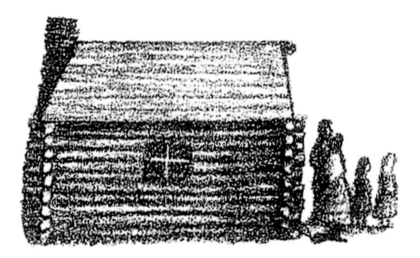

I Had a Little Nut Tree

BY MOTHER GOOSE

I had a little nut tree, nothing would it bear
But a silver apple and a golden pear;
The King of Spain's daughter came to see me,
And all for the sake of my little nut tree.
I skipped over water, I danced over sea,
And all the birds in the air couldn't catch me.

The Itsy Bitsy Spider

ANONYMOUS

The Itsy Bitsy Spider went up the waterspout.
Down came the rain and washed the spider out.
Out came the sun and dried up all the rain.
Now the Itsy Bitsy Spider went up the spout again.

I'm a Little Teapot

BY CLARENCE KELLY & GEORGE SANDERS

I'm a little teapot, short and stout.
Here is my handle; here is my spout.
When I get all steamed up, hear me shout!
Just tip me over and pour me out!

Little White Lily

BY GEORGE MACDONALD

Little White Lily sat by a stone,
Drooping and waiting till the sun shone.
Little White Lily sunshine has fed;
Little White Lily is lifting her head.

Little White Lily droopeth with pain,
Waiting and waiting for the wet rain.
Little White Lily holdeth her cup;
Rain is fast falling and filling it up.

Little White Lily said, "Good again,
When I am thirsty to have nice rain;
Now I am stronger, now I am cool;
Heat cannot burn me, my veins are so full!"

Little White Lily smells very sweet;
On her head sunshine, rain at her feet.
Thanks to the sunshine, thanks to the rain!
Little White Lily is happy again!

Block City

BY ROBERT LOUIS STEVENSON

What are you able to build with your blocks?
Castles and palaces, temples and docks.
Rain may keep raining, and others go roam,
But I can be happy and building at home.

Let the sofa be mountains, the carpet be sea,
There I'll establish a city for me:
A kirk and a mill and a palace beside.
And a harbor as well where my vessels may ride.

Now I have done with it, down let it go!
All in a moment the town is laid low.
Block upon block lying scattered and free,
What is there left of my town by the sea?

Yet as I saw it, I see it again,
The kirk and the palace, the ships and the men,
And as long as I live and where'er I may be,
I'll always remember my town by the sea.

Wynken, Blynken, and Nod

BY EUGENE FIELD

Wynken, Blynken, and Nod one night
Sailed off in a wooden shoe—
Sailed on a river of crystal light,
Into a sea of dew.
"Where are you going and what do you wish?"
The old moon asked the three.
"We have come to fish for the herring fish
That live in this beautiful sea.
Nets of silver and gold have we,"
said Wynken, Blynken, and Nod.

The old moon laughed and sang a song,
As they rocked in the wooden shoe,
And the wind that sped them all night long
Ruffled the waves of dew.
The little stars were the herring fish
That lived in that beautiful sea—
"Now cast your nets wherever you wish—
But never afraid are we."
So cried the stars to the fishermen three:
Wynken, Blynken, and Nod.

All night long their nets they threw
To the stars in the twinkling foam—
Then down from the skies came the wooden shoe,
Bringing the fishermen home;
'Twas all so pretty a sail, it seemed
As some folks thought 'twas a dream they'd dreamed
Of sailing the beautiful sea—

But I shall name you the fishermen three:
Wynken, Blynken, and Nod.

Wynken and Blynken are two little eyes,
And Nod is a little head.
And the wooden shoe that sailed the skies
Is a wee one's trundle bed.
So shut your eyes while mother sings
Of wonderful sights that be.
And you shall see the beautiful things
As you rock on the misty sea,
Where the old shoe rocked the fishermen three:
Wynken, Blynken, and Nod.

Goldilocks and the Three Bears

BY THE BROTHERS GRIMM

(Little Bear passage)

WHEN THE BIGGEST BEAR came to his porridge bowl, and found the spoon sticking upright, he knew at once that someone had meddled with it. So he gave an angry roar and growled in his big voice, "SOMEBODY HAS BEEN AT MY PORRIDGE!"

At this the Medium-sized Bear ran across the room to look at her breakfast; and when she found the spoon sticking up in her porridge bowl, she cried out, though not so loudly as the Biggest Bear had done, "SOMEBODY HAS BEEN AT MY PORRIDGE!"

Then the Little Bear ran to his porridge bowl; and when he found all his porridge gone, and not even enough left for the spoon to stand upright in, he squeaked in a poor, piteous little voice, "Somebody has been at *my* porridge, and has eaten it all up!"

He tilted up his little porridge bowl to show the others, stuffed his little forepaws into his little eyes, and began to cry.

The Little Mermaid

BY HANS CHRISTIAN ANDERSEN

FAR OUT AT SEA THE WATER is as blue as the petals of the prettiest cornflower and as clear as the purest glass. But it's very deep, deeper than any anchor can reach.

Down in the deepest spot of all is the castle of the sea king. Its walls are built of coral, and the long, pointed windows are made of the clearest amber.

The sea king had been a widower for some years, and his aged mother kept house for him. She was an intelligent woman, but proud when it came to her noble birth.

Otherwise, she deserved great praise, for she was very devoted to her grand-daughters, the little sea princesses. They were six pretty children, but the youngest was the loveliest of them all. Her skin was as clear and delicate as a rose leaf. Her eyes were as blue as the deepest sea.

All day long the sea princesses played in the great halls of the castle, where flowers grew right out of the walls. The large amber windows were open, and the fish swam in, just as swallows fly into our homes when we open the windows. The fish glided right up to the princesses, fed from their hands, and waited to be patted.

Outside the castle there was a beautiful garden with trees of deep blue and fiery red. Each of the little princesses had her own plot in the garden, where she could dig and plant as she pleased. While her sisters decorated their gardens with the wonderful things they obtained from sunken ships, the youngest

would have nothing but rose-red flowers that were like the sun high above, and a beautiful marble statue. The statue was of a handsome boy, chiseled from pure white stone, and it had come down to the bottom of the sea after a shipwreck.

Nothing pleased the princess more than to hear about the world of humans above the sea. Her old grandmother had to tell her all she knew of the ships and towns, the people and the animals.

"When you are fifteen," the grandmother told the princesses, "we will let you rise to the surface and sit in the moonlight while the great ships sail past. You will see both forests and towns."

None of the mermaids was more curious than the youngest, and she also had the longest wait. Many a night she stood at the open window and gazed up through the dark blue waters, where the fish splash with their fins and tails. She could see the moon and the stars, even though their light was rather pale.

Before the approach of a storm, when they expected a shipwreck, the sisters would swim in front of the vessel and sing sweetly of the delights to be found in the depths of the sea.

When the sisters floated up, arm in arm, through the water in this way, their youngest sister would always stay back all alone, gazing after them. She would have cried, but mermaids have no tears and suffer even more than we do. "Oh, if only I were fifteen years old," she would say. "I know that I will love the world up there and all the people who live in it."

Then, at last, she turned fifteen. She rose through the water as lightly and clearly as a bubble moves to the surface. The sun had just set as she lifted her head above the waves, but the clouds were still tinted with crimson and gold. Up in the pale, pink sky the evening star shone clear and bright. The air was mild and fresh, and the sea dead calm. A large three-masted ship was drifting in the water, with only one sail hoisted because not a breath of wind was stirring. The sailors were lolling about in the rigging and on the yards. There was music and singing on board, and when it grew dark, a hundred lanterns were lit. With their many colors, it looked as if the flags of all nations were fluttering in the air.

The Little Mermaid swam right up to the porthole of the cabin, and every time a wave lifted her up she could see a crowd of well-dressed people through the clear glass. Among them was a young prince, the handsomest person there, with large dark eyes. He could not have been more than sixteen. It was his birthday, and that's why there was so much of a stir. When the young prince came out on the deck, where the sailors were dancing, more than a hundred

rockets swished up into the sky and broke into a glitter, making the sky as bright as day.

The Little Mermaid was so startled that she dove down under the water. But she quickly popped her head out again. And look! It was just as if all the stars up in heaven were falling down on her. She had never seen fireworks. The ship itself was so brightly illuminated that you could see not only everyone there but even the smallest piece of rope. How handsome the young prince looked as he shook hands with the sailors! He laughed and smiled as the music sounded through the lovely night air.

It grew late, but the Little Mermaid could not take her eyes off the ship or the handsome prince. The colored lanterns had been extinguished; the rockets no longer rose in the air; and the cannon had ceased firing. But the sea had become restless, and you could hear a moaning, grumbling sound beneath the waves. Still, the mermaid stayed in the water, rocking up and down so that she could look into the cabin. The ship gathered speed; one after another of its sails was unfurled. The waves rose higher, heavy clouds darkened the sky, and lightning flashed in the distance. A dreadful storm was brewing. So the sailors took in the sails, while the great ship rocked and scudded through the raging sea. The waves rose higher and higher until they were like huge black mountains, threatening to bring down the mast.

The Little Mermaid suddenly realized that the ship was in danger. She herself had to be careful of the beams and bits of wreckage drifting in the water. One moment it was so dark that she could not see a thing, but then a flash of lightning lit up everyone on board. Now it was every man for himself. She was looking for the young prince, and, just as the ship was being torn apart, she saw him disappear into the depths of the sea. No, no, he must not die. So she swam in among the drifting beams and planks, oblivious to the danger of being crushed. She dove deep down and came right back up again among the waves, and at last she found the young prince. He could hardly swim any longer in the stormy sea. His limbs were failing him, his beautiful eyes were closed, and he would certainly have drowned if the Little Mermaid had not come to his rescue. She held his head above water and then let the waves carry her along with him.

By morning the storm had died down, and there was not a trace of the ship. The sun rose red and glowing up out of the water and seemed to bring color back into the prince's cheeks, but his eyes remained closed. The mermaid kissed his fine, high forehead and smoothed back his wet hair. He seemed to her like the marble statue in her little garden. She kissed him again and made a wish that he might live.

Soon the mermaid saw the mainland before her. The sea formed a small bay at this point, and the water in it was quite still, though very deep. The mermaid swam with the handsome prince to the beach, which was covered with fine, white sand. There she placed him in the warm sunshine, making a pillow for his head with the sand. Then she watched to see who would come to help the poor prince.

Not much later a young girl came along. When she saw the prince lying on the sand, she seemed quite frightened, but only for a moment, and ran to get help from others. The mermaid saw the prince come back to life, and he smiled at everyone around him. But there was no smile for her, because he had no idea that she had rescued him. After he was taken away, she felt so miserable that she dove into the water and returned to her father's palace.

She had always been silent and thoughtful, but now more so than ever. At length she could keep it to herself no longer and told one of her sisters everything. The others learned about it soon afterward. One of them was able to give her news about the prince. She, too, had seen the festival held on the ship and told the Little Mermaid about the prince and the location of his kingdom.

Now that the Little Mermaid knew where the prince had lived, she spent many an evening and many a night at that spot. She swam much closer to the shore than any of the others dared. She even went up the narrow channel to reach the fine marble balcony that threw its long shadow across the water. Here she would sit and gaze at the young prince, who thought he was completely alone in the bright moonlight.

On many nights when the fishermen were out at sea with their torches, she heard them praising the young prince, and their words made her even happier that she had saved his life the day he was drifting about half-dead on the waves. And she remembered how she had cradled his head on her chest and how lovingly she had kissed him.

The Little Mermaid grew more and more fond of human beings and longed deeply for their company. Their world seemed so much larger than her own. You see, they could fly across the ocean in ships and climb the steep mountains high above the clouds. And the lands they possessed, their woods and their fields, stretched far beyond where she could see. There was so much that she would have liked to know, and her sisters were not able to answer all her questions.

"We must be satisfied with what we have," said her grandmother. "Let's dance and be joyful. Tonight we are going to have a court ball."

That was something more splendid than anything we ever see on Earth. The walls and ceiling of the great ballroom were made of thick but transparent crystal. Through the middle of the ballroom flowed a broad stream, and in it mermen and mermaids were dancing to their own sweet song. No human beings have voices so lovely.

The Little Mermaid sang more sweetly than anyone else, and everyone applauded her. For a moment there was joy in her heart, for she knew that she had the most beautiful voice of anyone on land or in the sea. But then her thoughts turned to the world above her.

Suddenly, she caught the sound of a horn echoing through the water, and she thought: "Ah! There he is, sailing up above—he whom I love more than my father or my mother, he who is always in my thoughts and in whose hands I would gladly place my happiness. While my sisters are dancing away in Father's castle, I will go to the Sea Witch."

And so the Little Mermaid left her garden and set off for the place where the witch lived, on the far side of the foaming whirlpools. She had to pass through the middle of those churning eddies in order to get to the domain of the Sea Witch. The Little Mermaid came to a large slimy marsh in the wood, where big, fat water snakes were rolling in the mire, showing their hideous, whitish-yellow bellies. In the middle of the marsh stood a house, built with the bones of shipwrecked human folk. There sat the Sea Witch.

"I know exactly what you're after," said the Sea Witch. "You want to get rid of your fish tail and in its place have a couple of stumps to walk on like a human being so that the young prince will fall in love with you." And with that the witch let out a loud, repulsive laugh.

"I shall prepare a drink for you. You will have to swim to land with it before sunrise, sit down on the shore, and swallow it. Your tail will then divide in two and shrink into what human beings call 'pretty legs.'

"All who see you will say that you are the loveliest little human being they have ever seen. You will keep your graceful movements—no dancer will ever glide so lightly—but every step taken will make you feel as if you were treading on a sharp knife, enough to make your feet bleed. If you are prepared to endure all that, I can help you."

"Yes," said the Little Mermaid, and her voice trembled. But she turned her thoughts to the prince.

"Think about it carefully," said the witch. "If the prince marries someone else, the morning thereafter your heart will break, and you will become foam on the crest of the waves."

"I'm ready," said the Little Mermaid and she turned pale as death.

"But you will have to pay me," said the witch. "You're not getting my help for nothing. You have the loveliest voice of anyone who dwells down here at the bottom of the sea. You probably think that you can charm the prince with that voice, but you will have to give it to me. I am going to demand the best thing you possess as the price for my potion."

"But if you take away my voice," said the Little Mermaid, "what will I have left?"

"Your lovely figure," said the witch, "your graceful movements, and your expressive eyes. With those you can easily enchant a human heart . . . Well, where's your courage: Put out your little tongue and let me cut it off as my payment. Then you shall have your powerful potion."

"So be it," said the Little Mermaid, and the witch placed her cauldron on the fire to brew the magic potion. The witch kept tossing fresh things into the cauldron, and when the brew began to boil, it sounded like a crocodile weeping. At last the magic potion was ready, and it looked just like clear water.

"There you go," said the witch, as she cut off the Little Mermaid's tongue. The Little Mermaid was now dumb and could neither speak nor sing.

As she swam away the polyps shrank back in terror when they caught sight of the glittering potion that shone in her hand like a twinkling star. And so she passed quickly through the wood, the marsh, and the roaring whirlpools.

The Little Mermaid could see her father's palace. The lights in the ballroom were out. Everyone there was sure to be asleep by this time. But she did not dare to go in to see them, for now she was dumb and about to leave them forever. She felt as if her heart were going to break from grief.

The sun had not yet risen when she caught sight of the prince's palace and climbed the beautiful marble steps. The moon was shining clear and bright. The Little Mermaid drank the sharp, burning potion, and it seemed as if a double-

edged sword were passing through her delicate body. She fainted and fell down as if dead.

The sun rose and, shining across the sea, woke her up. She felt a sharp pain. But there in front of her stood the handsome young prince. He fixed his coal-black eyes on her so earnestly that she cast down her own and realized that her fish tail was gone and that she had as pretty a pair of white legs as any young girl could wish for. But she was quite naked and so she wrapped herself in her long, flowing hair. The prince asked who she was and how she had come there, and she could only gaze back at him sweetly and sadly with her deep blue eyes, for of course she could not speak. Then he took her by the hand and led her to the palace. Every step she took, as the witch had predicted, made her feel as if she were treading on sharp knives and needles, but she willingly endured it. She walked as lightly as a bubble by the prince's side. The prince and all who saw her marveled at the beauty of her graceful movements.

She was given costly dresses of silk and muslin after she arrived. She was the most beautiful creature in the palace, but she was dumb and could neither speak nor sing.

The prince presented her to his parents and seated her by his feet in the great hall. Beautiful slave girls dressed in silk and gold came out and danced before the prince and his royal parents.

The Little Mermaid raised her lovely white arms, stood on the tips of her toes, and glided across the floor, dancing as no one had danced before. Everyone was enchanted, especially the prince, who called her his little foundling. The prince said that she must never leave him, and she was given permission to sleep outside his door, on a velvet cushion.

"Ah, little does he know that it was I who saved his life," thought the Little Mermaid. "I carried him across the sea to the temple in the woods, and I waited in the foam for someone to come and help. I saw the pretty girl that he loves better than he loves me." And the mermaid sighed deeply, for she did not know how to shed tears. "He says the girl belongs to the holy temple and that she will therefore never return to the world. They will never again meet. I am by his side, and I see him every day. I will take care of him and love him and give up my life for him."

Not long after that, there was talk that the prince would marry and that the beautiful daughter of a neighboring king would be his wife, and that was why he was rigging out a splendid ship.

"I shall have to go," the prince told the Little Mermaid. "I have to visit this beautiful princess because my parents insist upon it. But they cannot force me to bring her back here as my wife. I could never love her. She is not at all like the beautiful girl in the temple, whom you resemble. If I were forced to choose a bride, I would rather choose you, my dear mute foundling, with the expressive eyes." And he kissed her rosy mouth, played with her long hair, and laid his head against her heart so that it dreamed of human happiness.

The next morning the ship sailed into the harbor of the neighboring king's magnificent capital. The church bells were ringing, and from the towers you could hear a flourish of trumpets. Soldiers saluted with gleaming bayonets and flying colors. Every day there was a festival. Balls and entertainments followed one another, but the princess had not yet appeared. People said that she was being brought up and educated in a holy temple, where she was learning all the royal virtues. At last she arrived.

The Little Mermaid was eager for a glimpse of her beauty, and she had to admit that she had never seen a more charming person. Her skin was clear and delicate, and behind long, dark eyelashes her laughing blue eyes shone with deep sincerity.

"It's you," said the prince to the princess. "You're the one who rescued me when I was lying half-dead on the beach." And he clasped his blushing bride in his arms.

"Oh, I am so very happy," he said to the Little Mermaid. "My dearest wish, more than I ever dared hope for, has been granted. My happiness will give you pleasure, because you're more devoted to me than anyone else." The Little Mermaid kissed his hand and she felt as if her heart were already broken. The day of his wedding would mean her death, and she would turn into foam on the ocean waves.

That same evening bride and bride-groom went on board the ship. The cannon roared, the flags were waving, and in the center of the ship a sumptuous tent of purple and gold had been raised. It was strewn with luxurious cushions, for the wedded couple was to sleep there on that calm, cool night. The sails filled with the breeze, and the ship glided lightly and smoothly over the clear seas. When it grew dark, colored lanterns were lit and the sailors danced merrily on deck. The Little Mermaid could not help thinking of that first time she had come up from the sea and gazed on just such a scene of joyous festivities. And now she joined in the dance, swerving and swooping as lightly as a swallow that avoids pursuit. Cries of admiration greeted her from all sides. Never before had she danced so elegantly. All was joy and merriment on board until long past midnight. She laughed and danced with the others while the thought of death was in her heart. The prince kissed his lovely bride, while she played with his dark hair, and arm in arm they retired to the magnificent tent.

The ship was hushed and quiet. Only the helmsman was there at his wheel. And the Little Mermaid leaned with her white arms on the rail and looked to the east for a sign of the rosy dawn. The first ray of sun, she knew, would bring her death. Suddenly she saw her sisters rising out of the sea. They were as pale as she, but their long, beautiful hair was no longer waving in the wind—it had been cut off.

"We have given our hair to the witch," they said, "to save you from the death that awaits you tonight. She has given us a knife—look, here it is. See how sharp it is? Before sunrise you must plunge it into the prince's heart. Then, when his warm blood splashes on your feet, they will grow back together and form a fish tail, and you will be a mermaid once more. Make haste! Either he or you will die before sunrise." And with a strange, deep sigh, they sank down beneath the waves.

The Little Mermaid drew back the purple curtain of the tent, and she saw the lovely bride sleeping with her head on the prince's chest. She bent down and kissed his handsome brow, then looked at the sky where the rosy dawn was growing brighter and brighter. She gazed at the sharp knife in her hand and again fixed her eyes on the prince, who whispered the name of his bride in his dreams—she alone was in his thoughts. The Little Mermaid's hand trembled as she held the knife—then she flung it far out over the waves.

With a last glance at the prince from eyes half-dimmed in death, she threw herself from the ship into the sea and felt her body dissolve into foam.

With a Little Help from My Friends

BY JOHN LENNON AND PAUL MCCARTNEY

(An excerpt)

What would you think if I sang out of tune,
Would you stand up and walk out on me?
Lend me your ears and I'll sing you a song
And I'll try not to sing out of key.

Oh I get by with a little help from my friends.
Oh I get by with a little help from my friends.
I'm gonna try with a little help from my friends.

A Teeny-Tiny Story

ANONYMOUS

ONCE UPON A TIME there lived a teeny-tiny woman in a teeny-tiny house in a teeny-tiny village. Now one day this teeny-tiny woman put on her teeny-tiny bonnet, and went out of her teeny-tiny house to take a teeny-tiny walk. And when this teeny-tiny woman had gone a teeny-tiny way, she saw a teeny-tiny doghouse, and outside the teeny-tiny doghouse was a teeny-tiny bone.

And the teeny-tiny woman said to her teeny-tiny self, "This teeny-tiny bone will make me some teeny-tiny soup for my teeny-tiny supper."

Now when the teeny-tiny woman got home to her teeny-tiny house, she was a teeny-tiny bit tired. She put the teeny-tiny bone into a teeny-tiny cupboard and went up her teen-tiny stairs to her teeny-tiny bed.

When this teeny-tiny woman had been asleep a teeny-tiny time, she was awakened by a teeny-tiny voice from the teeny-tiny cupboard, which said,

"Give me my bone!"

At this the teeny-tiny woman hid her teeny-tiny head under the teeny-tiny bedclothes. The teeny-tiny voice cried out again from the teeny-tiny cupboard a teeny-tiny bit louder,

"Give me my bone!"

The teeny-tiny woman hid her teeny-tiny head a teeny-tiny bit farther under the teeny-tiny bedclothes. But the teeny-tiny voice from the teeny-tiny cupboard said a teeny-tiny bit louder,

"Give me my bone!"

At this the teeny-tiny woman pulled her teeny-tiny head out of the teeny-tiny bedclothes, and said in her loudest teeny-tiny voice,

"TAKE IT!"

Little Fish

BY D. H. LAWRENCE

The tiny fish enjoy themselves
in the sea.
Quick little splinters of life,
their little lives are fun to them
in the sea.

The Lion and the Mouse

BY AESOP

A LION, TIRED FROM THE CHASE, lay sleeping at full length under a shady tree. Some mice, scrambling over him while he slept, awoke him. Laying his paw upon one of them, he was about to crush him, but the mouse begged for mercy so plaintively that he let him go. Some time later, the lion was caught in a net laid by some hunters and, unable to free himself, made the forest rumble with his angry roars. The mouse whose life had been spared came and, with his sharp little teeth, gnawed through the ropes, and set the lion free.

Moral
One good turn deserves another.

Fairy Bread

BY ROBERT LOUIS STEVENSON

Come up here, O dusty feet!
Here is fairy bread to eat.
Here is my retiring room,
Children, you may dine
On golden smell of broom
And the shade of pine;
And when you have eaten well,
Fairy stories hear and tell.

How Doth the Little Crocodile

BY LEWIS CARROLL

How doth the Little Crocodile
Improve his shining tail,
And pour the waters of the Nile
On every golden scale!

How cheerfully he seems to grin,
How neatly spreads his claws,
And welcomes little fishes in
With gently smiling jaws!

Cinderella

BY CHARLES PERRAULT

(Little Glass Slipper passage)

WHEN THE STEPSISTERS RETURNED, they were full of this strange adventure: how the beautiful lady had appeared at the ball more beautiful than ever and enchanted everyone who looked at her; and how as the clock was striking twelve, she had suddenly risen up and fled from the garden and through the ballroom, disappearing no one knew how or where, and dropping one of her little glass slippers behind her in her flight.

"The prince picked it up and has been looking at it and kissing it ever since," said the eldest sister, in a romantic tone. "All the court and the royal family are sure he is desperately in love with the wearer of the little glass slipper."

Thumbelina

BY HANS CHRISTIAN ANDERSEN

❦

(An excerpt)

THUS THEY CAME to the warm countries. There the sun shone much brighter than it does here; the heavens were twice as high, and upon trellis and hedge grew the most splendid purple and green grapes. Oranges and lemons hung golden in the woods, and myrtle and wild thyme sent forth their fragrance; the most beautiful children, on the highways, ran after and played with large, brilliantly colored butterflies. But the swallow still flew onward, and it became more and more beautiful. Among lovely green trees, and beside a beautiful blue lake, stood a palace, built of the shining white marble of antiquity. Vines clambered up the tall pillars; on the topmost of these were the swallows' nests, and in one of these dwelt the very swallow that carried Thumbelina.

"Here is my home!" said the swallow. "But wilt thou now seek out for thyself one of the lovely flowers which grow below, and then I will place thee there, and thou shalt make thyself as comfortable as thou pleasest?"

"That is charming!" said she, and clapped her small hands.

Just by there lay a large white marble pillar, which had fallen down, and broken into three pieces, but amongst these grew the most exquisite large white flowers.

The swallow flew down with Thumbelina, and seated her upon one of the broad leaves—but how amazed she was! There sat a little man in the middle of the flower, as white and transparent as if he were glass; the most lovely crown of gold was upon his head, and the most beautiful bright wings upon his shoulders, and he, too, was no larger than Thumbelina. He was the angel of the flower. In every flower lived such a little man or woman, but this was the king of them all.

"Good heavens! How small he is!" whispered Thumbelina to the swallow. The little prince was much frightened at the swallow, for it was, indeed, a great gigantic bird in comparison to him, who was so very small and delicate; but when he saw Thumbelina, he was very glad, for she was the prettiest little maiden that he had ever seen. He took, therefore, the golden crown from off his head, and set it upon hers, and asked her, what was her name, and whether she would be his wife, and be the queen of all the flowers? Yes, he was really and truly a little man, quite different from the frog's son, and from the mole, with his black velvet dress; she therefore said, "Yes," to the pretty prince; and so there came out of every flower a lady or a gentleman, so lovely that it was quite a pleasure to see them, and brought, every one of them, a present to Thumbelina; but the best of all was a pair of beautiful wings, of fine white pearl, and these were fastened on Thumbelina's shoulders, and thus she also could fly from flower to flower—that was such a delight! And the little swallow sat up in its nest and sang to them as well as it could, but still it was a little bit sad at heart, for it was very fond of Thumbelina, and wished never to have parted from her.

Twinkle, Twinkle, Little Star

BY JANE TAYLOR

Twinkle, twinkle, little star,
How I wonder what you are.
Up above the world so high,
Like a diamond in the sky.

When the blazing sun is gone,
When he nothing shines upon,
Then you show your little light,
Twinkle, twinkle, all the night.

Then the traveler in the dark
Thanks you for your tiny spark;
How could he see where to go,
If you did not twinkle so?

In the dark blue sky you keep,
Often through my curtains peep,
For you never shut your eye,
Till the sun is in the sky.

As your bright and tiny spark
Lights the traveler in the dark,
Though I know not what you are,
Twinkle, twinkle, little star.

The Little Land

BY ROBERT LOUIS STEVENSON

When at home alone I sit
And am very tired of it,
I have just to shut my eyes
To go sailing through the skies—
To go sailing far away
To the pleasant Land of Play;
To the fairy land afar
Where the Little People are;
Where the clover tops are trees,
And the rain pools are the seas
And the leaves like little ships
Sail about on tiny trips;
And above the daisy tree
Through the grasses,
High o'erhead the Bumble Bee
Hums and passes.

In that forest to and fro
I can wander, I can go;
See the spider and the fly,
And the ants go marching by
Carrying parcels with their feet
Down the green and grassy street.
I can climb the jointed grass
And on high
See the greater swallows pass
In the sky,
And the round sun rolling by
Heeding no such things as I.

Through that forest I can pass
Till, as in a looking glass,
Humming fly and daisy tree
And my tiny self I see,
Painted very clear and neat
On the rain pool at my feet.
Should a leaflet come to land
Drifting near to where I stand,
Straight I'll board that tiny boat
Round the rain pool sea to float.

Little thoughtful creatures sit
On the grassy coasts of it;
Little things with lovely eyes
See me sailing with surprise.
Some are clad in armor green
(These have sure to battle been!);
Some are pied with ev'ry hue,
Black and crimson, gold and blue;
Some have wings and swift are gone;
But they all look kindly on.

When my eyes I once again
Open, and see all things plain:
High bare walls, great bare floor;
Great big knobs on drawer and door:
Great big people perched on chairs,
Stitching tucks and mending tears,
Each a hill that I could climb,
And talking nonsense all the time—
O, dear me,
That I could be
A sailor on the rain pool sea,
A climber in the clover tree,
And just come back, a sleepyhead,
Late at night to go to bed.

Acknowledgments

We wish to thank the following properties whose cooperation has made this unique collection possible. All care has been taken to trace ownership of these selections and to make a full acknowledgment. If any errors or omissions have occured, they will be corrected in subsequent editions, provided notification is sent to the compiler.

Front Cover	Margaret Tarrant, from *In Wheelabout and Cockalone*, 1918.
Front Flap	Mabel Lucie Attwell, from *Alice's Adventures in Wonderland*, 1910.
Endpapers	Kate Greenway, from *The April Baby's Book of Tunes*, 1900.
Frontispiece	Eleanor Vere Boyle, from *Thumbelina*, 1872.
Title Page	William Donahey, from *Adventures of the Teenie Weenies*, 1920.
Copyright page	Jane Boyer, from *The Mary Frances Cook Book*, circa 1910.
Epigraph	Emily Benson Knipe, from *Forest-land*, 1905.
Preface	Harrison Weir, from *A Treasury of Pleasure Books for Young Children*, 1850.
11	Walter Satterlee, from *Mother Goose*, 1882.
12	Edward Julius Detmold, Loose ephemera, n.d.
13	Lois M. Murphy, from *With Scissors and Paste*, 1937.
14	Watty Piper, from *The Little Engine That Could*, 1930.
16	L. Leslie Brooke, from *Mother Goose*, 1922.
17	William Donahey, from *Adventures of the Teenie Weenies*, 1920.
18	Grandville, from *Voyages de Gulliver*, 1838.
19	Unknown, from *McLoughlin Brother's Gulliver's Travels in Brobdingnag*, 1880.
21	Hardie Gramatsky, from *Little Toot*, 1939.
22	Palmer Cox, from *The Brownie ABC*, 1895.
23	Kate Greenway, from *The April Baby's Book of Tunes*, 1900.
24	John Hassall, from *Mother Goose's Book of Nursery Stories, Rhymes and Fables*, 1928.